W9-CQJ-725

NOAH & THE ARK & THE ANIMALS

Andrew Clements
Ivan Gantschev

NOAH & THE ARK & THE ANIMALS

SCHOLASTIC INC.
New York   Toronto   London   Auckland   Sydney

The colt looked out through the open doorway at the gray sky, the flooded pasture, and the muddy barnyard.

The autumn rain had been falling for three days now, rapping day and night upon the tin roof of the barn. He leaned against the warm dappled flank of his mother and restlessly stamped his hooves.

"When will all this rain stop? Is it going to just pour and pour forever?" he asked. The wise old mare sniffed the breeze.

"All I smell is rain and more rain, but I know that it will not go on long enough to do us any harm."

The colt gave a little snort that sent two small clouds of steam down into the cold damp air. "Well, I think it's going to rain for weeks and weeks, and we'll all be washed away!"

His mother nudged him toward their stall in the barn, and said, "Come and lie down next to me, and I will tell you how I know that the rain will stop."

When they were both settled into the fragrant hay, the mare began her story.

Long, long ago, there were people and
animals living on the earth, just as they
do today. The animals lived as they were
supposed to, but the people started to do
things wrong. And so, God was very
disappointed with all of the people—
except one. His name was Noah.
When other men lied and stole from each other,
Noah was honest, and he taught his children
to be the same way. When other men fought and
hurt each other, Noah and his family kept to their
own work, cheerful and happy and good.
And when other men prayed to statues
and trees, Noah's family prayed to God.
God could tell that Noah was a man
He could trust.

God told Noah that a great flood would come to wash away all the people who had forgotten how to be good, a flood that would clean up the whole earth.
At first, Noah was very sad at this news, but God had a plan to save Noah's family and all the animals.

God told Noah that he must build an ark. The ark would be a floating barn for all the different kinds of animals, and a houseboat for Noah and his family.

God gave Noah instructions for building the ark. There was a lower deck, a middle deck and an upper deck in the ark. There were rooms for the people, a big doorway on the side, and one window up near the roof. When Noah had finished building the ark God told him to cover the inside and the outside with tar to keep out the water.

Building the ark was a big job, but the next job was even bigger.
God told Noah to bring a male and a female of every kind of living
creature into the ark, and then to make sure that there was enough
food to feed them all for a long time.
Noah probably did not know it, but at the same time God was
telling him to look for all those creatures, God was also
telling all the creatures to look for Noah.
That made the job a little easier.

First, Noah brought in all the animals that walked on the earth.
There were cows and horses and goats and sheep, rabbits and
monkeys and wolves and mice, camels and elephants,
pigs and apes, jackals and donkeys and weasels and cats,
giraffes and grizzly bears, lions and dogs —
to name just a few.

Then Noah gathered up the birds that flew above the earth.
There were eagles and pigeons and storks and loons, sparrows and herons,
flamingoes and hawks, peacocks and pelicans, warblers and larks, parrots and condors
and chickens and ducks, woodpeckers, ostriches, linnets and swans—
to mention one or two.

And finally Noah even had to make
room for the reptiles and the insects
that crawled on the earth.
There were lizards and grasshoppers,
turtles and worms, snakes and beetles
and spiders and ants, aphids and
butterflies, snails and frogs, fireflies,
bumblebees, june bugs and fleas—
and the tiny ones that could not fly
just hopped onto a bird or animal
and rode right on board.

As soon as the last creatures and supplies had come into the ark, the Lord closed the door and the rain bega

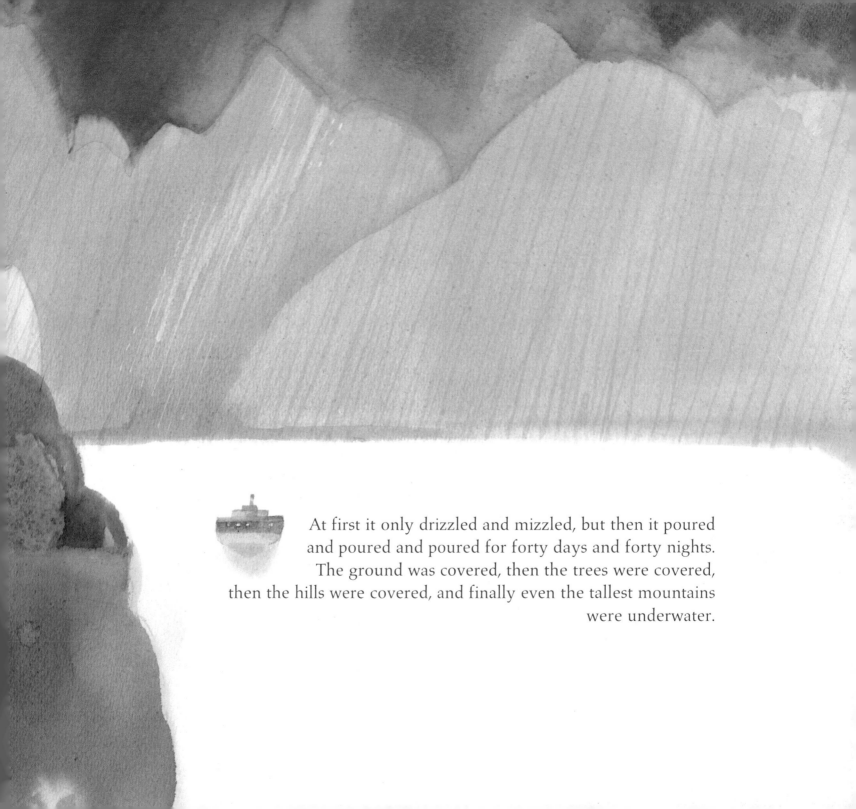

At first it only drizzled and mizzled, but then it poured and poured and poured for forty days and forty nights. The ground was covered, then the trees were covered, then the hills were covered, and finally even the tallest mountains were underwater.

The water covered the earth for one hundred and fifty days!
That is a very long time to be swaying around in a floating barn.
But God did not forget Noah and the creatures in the ark.
He sent a great wind blowing on the earth, and the water began to dry up.

One morning Noah woke up and found that the ark was sitting on top of a mountain called Ararat. When he looked out of the window, Noah could not tell if it was safe to open the door or not. So he took a dove and let it fly away to explore the earth.

That night, the dove came back to the ark, so Noah knew that there was still no other dry place for the dove to rest or eat.

Seven days later, Noah let the dove fly away again, and again it came back, but this time it had a branch from an olive tree in its beak.

One week later Noah let the dove fly off for the third time, and this time it did not come back. Noah was sure now that it was safe to go out, so he opened the door of the ark.

Then God said something to Noah and his family and to all the other creatures who came out of the ark that day. God said that they should all go out into the whole world to have families and to replenish the earth. He also told them all to obey God's laws. And God promised Noah and all the other living creatures that there would never be another great flood. Then He put a rainbow in the sky as a sign to remind all the earth of the promise and of His love for every living creature.

When the mare finished telling the story, it was very quiet in the barn.
All the other animals had gathered around the stall to listen and remember.
But it was extra quiet, because something else had happened too: the rain had stopped!
The colt and the mare and everyone else went to the door and looked out over the fields and
meadows. The clouds were breaking up, the sunlight was peeking through, and above the hills
at the end of the valley was a rainbow.
"Does that mean that God is keeping the promise?" asked the colt. The mare nodded her head.

The colt stood quietly for a moment. "Well, I want to go out now," he said.
"But I'm going to remember about Noah, and I won't forget about God's promise even if it
rains every day for a whole week."
And the colt ran off to splash in the puddles.

No part of this publication may be reproduced in whole or in part,
or stored in a retrieval system, or transmitted in any form or
by any means, electronic, mechanical, photocopying, recording,
or otherwise, without written permission of the publisher.
For information regarding permission, write to Picture Book Studio,
10 Central Street, Saxonville, MA 01701.

ISBN 0-590-44457-3

Text copyright © 1984 by Picture Book Studio.
Illustrations copyright © 1984 by Neugebauer Press, Salzburg.
All rights reserved. Published by Scholastic Inc., 730 Broadway,
New York, NY 10003, by arrangement with Picture Book Studio.

BLUE RIBBON is a registered trademark of Scholastic Inc.

12 11 10 9 8 7 6 5 4 3   5 6 7/9

Printed in the U.S.A.   08

First Scholastic printing, March 1992